Silky the Fairy enters the Land of Mine-All-Mine from the Faraway Tree looking for adventure. She has visited many Lands in search of fun and excitement. But when she meets Talon the evil Troll she soon finds that her Enchanted World is turned upside down.

To rescue the Talismans that have been lost from the Faraway Tree, Silky will need some help, and fast! Luckily she can rely on her best fairy friends to help her in her task. With the special talents of Melody, Petal, Pinx and Bizzy, Silky must save the Lands of the Enchanted World. But will the fairies succeed or will Talon get his evil ~~~

EGMONT

We bring stories to life

Melody and the Enchanted Harp
Published in Great Britain 2008
by Egmont UK Limited
239 Kensington High Street, London W8 6SA

Text and illustrations © 2008 Enid Blyton Ltd, a Chorion
company
Text by Elise Allen
Illustrations by Pulsar Studio (Beehive Illustration)

ISBN 978 1 4052 4255 4

1 3 5 7 9 10 8 6 4 2

A CIP catalogue record for this title is available from
the British Library

Printed and bound in Great Britain by the CPI Group

JF

Enid Blyton's ENCHANTED WOORLD

Melody and the Enchanted Harp

by Elise Allen

EGMONT

Meet the Faraway Fairies

Favourite Colour — Yellow. It's a beautiful colour that reminds me of sunshine and happiness.

Talent — Light. I can release rays of energy to light up a room or, if I really try hard, I can use it to break out of tight situations. The only problem is that when I lose my temper I can have a 'flash attack' which is really embarrassing because my friends find it funny.

Favourite Activity — Exploring. I love an adventure, even when it gets me into trouble. I never get tired of visiting new places and meeting new people.

Favourite Colour — Blue. The colour of the sea and the sky. I love every shade from aquamarine to midnight blue.

Talent — As well as being a musician I can also transform into other objects. I like to do it for fun, but it also comes in useful if there's a spot of bother.

Favourite Activity — Singing and dancing. I can do it all day and never get tired.

Favourite Colour – Green. It's the colour of life. All my best plant friends are one shade of green or another.

Talent – I can speak to the animals and plants of the Enchanted World . . . not to mention the ones in the Faraway Tree.

Favourite Activity – I love to sit peacefully and listen to the constant chatter of all creatures, both big and small.

Favourite Colour – Pink. What other colour would it be? Pink is simply the best colour there is.

Talent – Apart from being a supreme fashion designer, I can also become invisible. It helps me to escape from my screaming fashion fans!

Favourite Activity – Designing. Give me some fabrics and I'll make you something fabulous. Remember – If it's not by Pinx . . . your makeover stinks!

Favourite Colour – Orange. It's the most fun colour of all. It's just bursting with life!

Talent – Being a magician of course. Although I have been known to make the odd Basic Bizzy Blunder with my spells.

Favourite Activity – Baking Brilliant Blueberry Buns and Marvellous Magical Muffins. There is always time to bake a tasty cake to show your friends that you care.

www.blyton.com/enchantedworld

Contents

Introduction		1
Chapter One	Calm in Chaos	4
Chapter Two	The Land of Music	17
Chapter Three	Allegra	29
Chapter Four	The Game	41
Chapter Five	Queen Quadrille	52
Chapter Six	The Golden Cage	62
Chapter Seven	The Soundless Pit	69
Chapter Eight	Melody or the Harp	83
Chapter Nine	Talon's Return	97
Chapter Ten	Melody Plays The Game	105
Chapter Eleven	Rise of the Queen	118
Chapter Twelve	Allegra's Message	133
Sneak Preview Chapter		144

Introduction

*T*ucked away among the thickets, groves and
forests of our Earth is a special wood. An
Enchanted Wood, where the trees grow taller, the
branches grow stronger and the leaves grow denser
than anywhere else. Search hard enough within this
Enchanted Wood, and you'll find one tree that
towers above all the others. This is the Faraway Tree,
and it is very special. It is home to magical creatures
like elves and fairies, even a dragon. But the most
magical thing about this very magical Tree? It is the
sole doorway to the Lands of the Enchanted World.

Most of the time, the Lands of the Enchanted
World simply float along, unattached to anything.
But at one time or another, they each come to rest at

the top of the Faraway Tree. And if you're lucky enough to be in the Tree at the time, you can climb to its very top, scramble up the long Ladder extending from its tallest branch, push through the clouds and step into that Land.

Of course, there's no telling when a Land will come to the Faraway Tree, or how long it will remain. A Land might stay for months, or be gone within the hour. And if you haven't made it back down the Ladder and into the Faraway Tree before the Land floats away, you could be stuck for a very long time. This is scary even in the most wonderful of Lands, like the Land of Perfect Birthday Parties. But if you get caught in a place like the Land of Ravenous Toothy Beasts, the situation is absolutely terrifying. Yet even though exploring the Lands has its perils, it's also exhilarating, which is why creatures from all over the Enchanted World (and the occasional visiting human) come to live in the Faraway Tree so they can travel from Land to Land.

Of course, not everyone explores the Lands for

pleasure alone. In fact, five fairies have been asked
do so for the ultimate cause: to save the life of the
Faraway Tree and make sure that the doorway to the
Enchanted World remains open. These are their
stories . . .

Chapter One

Calm in Chaos

'AAAHHH!' wailed Pinx as a fierce blast of wind blew a flurry of butterblooms off the dress she was creating for Petal, who was standing patiently on Pinx's fitting pedestal.

'Silky!' Pinx huffed as she flew around the room after the flowers, 'I just pinned those on!'

'Sorry, Pinx!' Silky cried over her shoulder, but she was already far across the main room of the fairies' treehouse, riding behind Zuni on the back of Misty the Unicorn.

As Misty soared through the air, her mighty wings beat gust after gust. Although that caused a problem for Pinx, it was heavenly for Silky. She loved the feeling of the wind streaking through her long, blonde hair as Zuni urged Misty to dive, twirl and perform all her most impressive tricks.

'This one's brand new,' Zuni grinned.

Silky screamed with delight as Misty executed a perfect loop-the-loop, the wind from which sent the butterblooms flying all over again. Pinx's face turned as pink as her zigzag pigtails as she roared in frustration, which of course made Petal laugh out loud.

'Oh, Pinx, it's OK,' Petal said in her most soothing voice. 'Let me help.'

She flew off the platform to chase the blooms. But although the two fairies tried, it was impossible to chase down all the butterblooms that filled the room. Several blooms floated down to Bizzy, who was very carefully opening the oven door. Her wild, black curls were spattered with dabs of flour, butter and spellulose, her secret ingredient for Magical Message Muffins, which she had been trying unsuccessfully to bake all day.

'I think the key,' said Bizzy as she gingerly

took out the twelfth muffin pan of the afternoon, 'is to be silent and still while I say the final spell. Muffle-wuffle-rise-n-puff– AAAAH!'

A flurry of butterblooms floated down from above, followed closely by a swooping twosome of Petal and Pinx.

'I've got them!' both fairies shouted.

Bizzy looked up to see her friends dive-bombing towards her, screamed and raised the muffin tin above her head like a shield – a motion that sent the muffins springing out of the tin and on to the floor.

Muffins on the floor were an irresistible treat to the crowd of birds, squirrels and other small animals that liked to stay close to Petal. Just as the birds lunged for the muffins, Bizzy's improperly finished spell took effect, turning the treats into a dozen *puffins*.

The puffins squawked angrily, and then waddled and flew around the room, eagerly

searching for any morsels of fish.

This was life in the Faraway Fairies'
treehouse. Ever since Silky had gathered her
best friends to live in the Faraway Tree and
join her on a mission to retrieve its life-
giving Talismans, every day was a whirlwind
of giddy chaos, with friends like Zuni and
Misty, not to mention a rotating menagerie
of Petal's animal friends coming round to

join in the excitement.

Only one fairy seemed completely serene in the midst of the insanity. Melody floated in the middle of the room and danced, unaffected by Misty's tricks, the snowstorm of blooms or even the sudden appearance of puffins.

'One, two . . .' she counted as she performed a perfect pirouette, moved into an arabesque and then did a double scissor-kick. Without missing a beat of the song lilting through her head, she deftly ducked out of the way of Misty, who was still carrying Zuni and Silky through her favourite tricks.

'Sorry about that, Melody,' Zuni called, but Melody didn't respond.

'Melody?' Silky said.

Melody didn't answer her either. She just screwed up her green eyes, concentrating even harder, then flew straight up in the air and spun around ten times in a row – a decuple twirliette – an almost unheard-of achievement among Twinkletune Fairies. Melody's friends would have been stunned if they had noticed, but none of them had. Melody didn't mind. She just allowed herself a small smile and then turned her attention back to Silky and Zuni.

'Sorry, everyone,' Melody said. 'I just wanted to make the step perfect.'

Pinx and Petal had finished gathering up the butterblooms and Pinx was back to working on her latest masterpiece, but she turned to Melody with a grimace.

'I don't get it,' she declared. 'If you need to concentrate, why not practise in your room?'

But Melody was already working on another dance routine, and sang out her answer to the tune running through her head: 'I dance my best when I'm happy, and I'm at my happiest when I'm with all of you.'

Bizzy used her foot to close the oven door on her latest muffin attempt and then grabbed a puffin, adding it to the squawking foursome already wriggling in her arms.

'But aren't we a Dilly of Decided Distractions?' she asked.

As if to prove her point, a puffin squirmed out of her grasp and flew straight at Melody, who grabbed it by its wings.

'You're not *very* distracting,' Melody declared, incorporating the puffin into her dance by spinning it twice around before giving it a deep dip. 'Besides,' she continued, twirling the puffin back to Bizzy, 'I can do anything I set my mind to.'

There was something in Melody's voice as she spoke that made Silky pay attention. It was a determination. Silky had heard it in her friend before, even when they were kids, but Melody had such a happy-go-lucky nature that it was easy to forget this other side of her. Intrigued, Silky flew off Misty's back to take a closer look. She saw the same Melody as always: long orange ponytail, open green eyes and that straight-backed stance that Silky had always attributed to years of dancing. But now that she thought about it, maybe Melody's posture wasn't just training. Maybe it was a sign of her inner steel.

Silky smiled, looking at her friend with new admiration, but before she could say anything, there was a knock at the door. Silky opened it to reveal an enormous head teetering on a tiny body. The head was dominated by a shockingly large nose that ran all the way from the top of the forehead to the bottom of the chin, and two radar-dish ears that rotated quickly, picking up every sound within range. This was Cluecatcher, and there was only one reason why he would show up at the treehouse with such an anxious look in his eight eyes. Silky lit up with excitement.

'There's a new Land coming to the top of the Tree!' she gasped.

A wrinkled old woman cloaked in black

stepped out from behind Cluecatcher.

'Yes, there is,' Witch Whisper confirmed.

She stepped inside with Cluecatcher as all the other fairies stopped what they were doing to gather around.

'It's the Land of Music,' Witch Whisper

continued, 'and its Talisman is the Enchanted Harp.'

Melody gasped audibly.

'The Land of Music?' she cried. 'But I can't –'

Melody suddenly seemed to realise that everyone was looking at her in concern. She forced a smile and tried to sound positive.

'I can't wait!' she continued. 'I've always *dreamed* of visiting the Land of Music.'

She must have sounded convincing as everyone turned back to Witch Whisper. Everyone except Silky. Melody smiled wider to show her friend that she was fine.

'You all understand what's at stake,' Witch Whisper continued. 'The Talismans that tie the Faraway Tree to each Land of the Enchanted World must be returned to our Vault. They are the Tree's life force. Without them, the Tree will die. And if they fall into the wrong hands . . .'

'*Talon's* hands,' Pinx interrupted venomously.

She still hadn't forgiven the evil Troll for ruining the dress that she had made for Princess Twilleria's Sweet Centennial Ball.

'He'll be after the Harp,' Witch Whisper warned. 'He's desperate to control the gateway to the Enchanted World.'

DING!

'Oh!' Bizzy cried, and zipped back to the oven, where she gingerly removed the muffin tin, closed her eyes and concentrated, chanting, 'Muffle-wuffle-rise-n-puffle!'

POOF! The muffins puffed up to twice their size.

'It worked!' Bizzy cheered. 'And now we can finally read our Majorly Monumental Magic Muffin Message!'

She ripped open a piping-hot muffin and pulled out a small scroll from inside. Bizzy managed to unroll the warm note and read it aloud: 'Tread lightly where you don't belong, lest sorrow be your only song.'

Pinx wrinkled up her nose.

'What does that mean?' she asked.

'It means . . .' Melody began nervously, but an excited Bizzy cut her off.

'It means we shouldn't be Hopelessly Hapless Homebodies when we have a Massively Momentous Mission in the Land of Music!' she cried. 'Let's go!'

Bizzy flew off towards the Ladder at the top of the Tree, with the other fairies following close behind. Melody came last, and when Silky turned, she could see that her friend's normally pale face had turned absolutely white. Silky flew close to Melody.

'Is everything OK?' she asked gently.

As soon as Melody heard Silky's concern, she banished all doubt from her face.

'It's great!' Melody beamed. 'I'm right behind you.'

But Silky wasn't reassured. Something about the Land of Music was bothering

Melody horribly, but *what*? What could be so terrible that Melody couldn't share it with her closest friends?

Chapter Two

The Land of Music

The sound hit them as soon as they entered the Land. Music.

Given that they were in the Land of Music, it wasn't all that surprising. But the depth of the music was what struck the fairies – it came from everywhere. Tones and overtones; deep, throaty woodwinds; high tinkling chimes; lilting strings and strident brass, and under it all the thumping percussion bringing it all together. It was a musical feast and as the fairies flew along, savouring the sounds, they suddenly realised . . .

'It's coming from everything,' Silky marvelled. 'Everything is an instrument.'

A field of bluebells was, on closer inspection, an actual field of *blue bells*, pealing out a

tuneful refrain. What looked like a sea of reeds was actually made of recorders, tooting alongside a brook that not only babbled, but also sang along in perfect harmony. Even the clouds above breathed like accordions, groaning their chords as they billowed in and out.

'It's beautiful,' Bizzy said in wonder.

'It's pretty,' Pinx agreed. 'But who *lives* here?'

'Pinx!' Petal objected, then turned and cried out to the surrounding instruments. 'She didn't mean it. She knows that plants are as alive as any other creatures, and I bet she's going to apologise right now.'

Pinx's face lit up.

'Yes! That's an excellent idea!' she exclaimed.

Petal smiled . . . until Pinx eagerly continued speaking.

'Talk to the plants and ask them where all the *real* creatures are,' Pinx finished.

A giggle exploded out of Bizzy before she could clap her hands over her mouth to stop it. Silky almost laughed too, but Petal just looked at them open-mouthed and then turned her back on them completely.

Silky flew over to her friend.

'Petal, don't take it too seriously,' she said. 'It's Pinx. She's just teasing you.'

Petal shook her head.

★ ★ ★ 19 ★ ★ ★

'It's not that,' she said, 'it's the song . . .'

Petal was still for a moment, listening.

'I thought at first that the Land was singing to welcome us, but all the instruments are still singing the same song,' she said slowly. 'Every one – they just sing it over and over.'

'Maybe it's their favourite,' Bizzy suggested.

'*All* of them?' said Petal. 'It doesn't make sense. Every living thing should have its own song, but here they don't. They just sing . . .' Petal listened again to make sure that she got the words right. '"We hail our Queen with boundless zeal, that gift of music Queen Quad . . . Quad . . ." I can't make it out.'

'Queen Quadrille,' Melody intoned.

They were the first words she had spoken since they had arrived in the Land of Music. The other fairies all turned to see her unusually sombre face.

'OK Melody, start talking,' Pinx said, her hands on her hips.

'What do you mean?' asked Melody, not meeting her eyes.

'You've been acting strangely ever since we found out about the Land of Music,' Pinx said. 'What's the matter?'

Melody glanced up at her four best friends. She really didn't want to tell them, but they all looked so concerned. Finally, she took a deep breath and then began to explain.

'For years, the finest singers and musicians in the Enchanted World have been invited to come to the Land of Music to study in a Conservatory under Queen Quadrille,' said Melody. 'It's every Twinkletune Fairy's dream. My own great-great-grandmother, Soprana, was invited to study with the tenth Queen Quadrille, but ...'

Her voice trailed off. She couldn't finish.

Bizzy winced sympathetically. 'But you've never been invited?' she said.

Melody shook her head. Everyone was

silent, feeling Melody's deep humiliation. Everyone except Pinx . . .

'That's *it*?' Pinx said incredulously. 'Don't worry! You are the most fantabulous singer and musician in the entire Enchanted World, and if Queen Quad-a-what-*ever* can't hear it, she's tone deaf!'

'But –' objected Melody.

Pinx held up her hand and fixed Melody with a meaningful look.

'I'd stake my reputation on it,' she said.

Melody smiled. She knew better than to argue. Even though Pinx could seem harsh sometimes, her friends always knew that she was telling them exactly what she felt.

'Huge Hearty Happy-Hug!' cried Bizzy.

All four of the other fairies grinned and zoomed towards Melody, piling into her arms and knocking her off balance until the whole tangled lot of them tumbled backwards and landed in a giggling heap.

'Silky – your necklace!' Bizzy cried.

When Silky held up the crystal heart around her neck, she saw that it was blushing a faint shade of pink. Witch Whisper had given her the crystal necklace to help her locate the Talismans. The closer she got to a Talisman, the redder the crystal would grow.

'The Enchanted Harp,' smiled Silky. 'It must be this way. Come on.'

Silky led the group over a multicoloured field of humming kazoo grass dotted with grazing cowbells. As she flew, she held the crystal, watching its blush grow ever deeper.

'Wait!' Melody called suddenly.

The other fairies turned to see Melody hovering perfectly still, concentrating on something.

'I hear a song,' she said.

'Um . . . yes,' Pinx said, rolling her eyes, 'Everything here is singing.'

'No,' Melody said, 'it's different. Something's

singing a different song from the rest of the Land.' Her whole face softened as she listened, and she did a sudden pirouette as she sighed, 'It's beautiful.'

As if pulled by the music itself, Melody soared off to find its source.

'The Talisman's *this* way!' Silky cried.

But it was no use. For Melody, even a Talisman was no match for truly beautiful music. She triple-twirled, glowing with happiness, beckoned for her friends to follow her and then disappeared over a hill.

Silky shook her head, flustered.

'I don't believe this,' she huffed.

'I think it's good we're checking it out,' Petal said. 'It could be the only unique song in the entire Land of Music.'

This may have been true, but it had absolutely nothing to do with the Talisman, and between Talon and the habit Lands had of moving away from the top of the Faraway

Tree, Silky hated to waste a single second.

'Psst!' Melody hissed, cutting into Silky's thoughts.

Melody was crouching among a patch of bushes that were covered in finger-cymbal flowers. She put a finger to her lips to warn them to be quiet as they squeezed in beside her. Silky, Petal and Pinx slipped in easily, but Bizzy paused, trying to work out how to fold herself silently in between the cymbals.

'I think I need some help,' she whispered. 'Hello?'

But Pinx, Petal and Silky were already peering through a gap in the branches to see the source of Melody's excitement. Dancing in the middle of a clearing was a girl, but one unlike any creature they had ever seen. Her blonde curls were wind chimes, tinkling with every move. Her hollow, tube-like tongue flicked in and out, dancing along the musical scale like a slide whistle. Her fingers ended in

tiny, round castanets and she had a long, mallet-shaped tail that she used to beat on her bass-drum belly and gong-like back. Her shoulders rattled like maracas and, above it all, rose her gorgeous, lilting voice.

'Can you believe it?' Melody whispered. 'She's a living orchestra!'

The four friends were mesmerised by the girl, and even Silky could have stood there listening to her all day, but by this time Bizzy had become quite frustrated by trying to find a silent way into the finger-cymbal bushes.

'Oh, bother it,' she muttered.

She squeezed shut her eyes and dived into the copse, setting off a racket of CLANGs and CLINGs and TINKLE-JANGs and CHINGs as a bush reverberated with her crash entrance.

'Oops,' Bizzy said, as the others turned on her.

Melody, however, focused only on the living orchestra, who gasped in shock at the sound of

Bizzy's crash, and immediately started to flee.

'Wait!' cried Melody, stepping out of the bushes. 'That song, it was –'

'AAAHHH!' screamed the musical girl.

She curled into a ball on the ground.

'Please don't take me away!' she begged. 'I promise I'll never do it again! Please!'

Melody's jaw dropped. What had she done wrong? How had she made this girl so horribly frightened?

Chapter Three

Allegra

Silky was the first to overcome her surprise.
She flew to the musical girl's side.

'It's OK,' she said gently, placing a
reassuring hand on the girl's shoulder. 'No
one's taking you anywhere.'

The girl looked up at them with scared
eyes, her curls chiming as they fell to one side.

'You mean . . . you're not with the Queen?'
she asked.

'No, we're not,' Melody quickly murmured.

'Thank goodness,' said the girl, and her
whole body rattled and jangled as she
clambered to her feet. 'My name's Allegra.'

'I'm Silky. And these are my friends Pinx,
Petal, Bizzy and Melody.'

The girls said hello, but Melody couldn't

contain her excitement.

'We'd love it if you'd sing again,' she burst
out. 'I've never heard anything like it. Do I
have the tune right?'

Melody paused for a moment, listening for
the notes in her head, and then gave a perfect
rendition of Allegra's song.

After growing up with Melody, and more
recently living with her almost constant peals
of song, her friends sometimes took her
unusually exquisite voice for granted. But if
they needed any reminder of its splendour,
they only had to look at Allegra, who stared
at Melody in open-mouthed awe.

'Don't stop!' she squealed when Melody
paused. 'Your voice! It's so –'

Allegra suddenly looked frightened again,
peering around, as if searching for
eavesdroppers.

'No,' she corrected herself. 'Stop. I don't
want you to get in trouble because of me.'

'In trouble for singing?' Pinx asked sceptically. 'In the Land of *Music*?'

'Yes!' cried Allegra.

She looked around again and then lowered her voice.

'Queen Quadrille only lets us sing "Hail to Queen Quadrille",' she continued. 'If we're caught singing anything else she makes us play The Game.'

'Really?' bubbled Bizzy. 'What kind of game? Hollyhock Hopscotch? Upside-down Twiddle Tag? Ooh – how about Piddelywinks? I'm Practically Perfect at Piddleywinks!'

Allegra shook her head, her face pale.

'You don't want to play Queen Quadrille's Game,' she said gravely.

'But Queen Quadrille adores music,' Melody objected. 'She'd never punish anyone for singing what's in their heart.'

'Maybe that was true with other Queen Quadrilles, but not this one,' said Allegra. 'The minute her mother stepped down, this Queen Quadrille changed everything.'

'And nobody stood up to her?' asked Pinx. 'Because believe me, if Princess Twilleria tried something like that in Fairyland, there's no way I'd let it happen.'

'We tried at first,' Allegra said, shaking her head. 'But whenever anyone confronted her, she just played her harp and the next thing they knew, they were back outside the castle, with no idea how they got there, and no desire to go back and fight. At least, those were the lucky ones. The others . . .'

Allegra gulped and shook her head, as if not wanting to fathom what had happened to the others.

'Now most of us are too afraid to try,' she finished.

Silky, Bizzy, Pinx, Petal and Melody all exchanged looks, a gleam lighting their eyes. If Queen Quadrille enchanted her subjects with a harp, it could mean only one thing.

'You have to take us to Queen Quadrille,' Silky said.

Allegra's eyes grew wide with horror.

'Maybe you didn't understand –' she began.

Silky interrupted and explained that the fate of the entire Enchanted World depended on them retrieving the Enchanted Harp and returning it to the Faraway Tree.

But Allegra still shook her head warily.

'I see what you're saying,' she began, 'but going to Queen Quadrille . . . I just don't know . . .'

Without a sound, Melody flew over and landed next to Allegra. She slipped a comforting arm around the girl and sang to her softly. Her song was nothing more than the word 'Please', but she let the word roll and trill over several octaves, embracing Allegra with its soothing tone. Allegra visibly softened as the song went on. When it was over, she gently smiled at Melody.

'I'll do it,' she said. 'I could never say no to a voice like that. Come on – I'll take you through the catacombs; it's the fastest way.'

'Amazing,' Pinx whispered to Silky as they all followed Allegra into a towering forest of bagpipes. 'An entire Land where they make decisions the same way as Melody.'

Allegra reached a large patch of cymbals that grew close to the ground, mushroom-like. She glanced around nervously, then lifted one up to reveal a hole. She slipped inside, motioning for the fairies to follow.

When the fairies followed Allegra, they found themselves in an underground cavern. Here the constant renditions of 'Hail to Queen Quadrille' faded to a dim whisper, and the fairies were stunned by the sudden near-silence.

'This way,' said Allegra.

She led them through a series of tunnels.

'These catacombs are all over the Land of
Music,' Allegra explained. 'A group of us called
the Countermeasures built them when we
realised that we couldn't stop Queen
Quadrille. These days, when you believe in
freedom of song, you need ways to escape
quickly.'

The catacombs branched constantly, a
maze of shadowy passages leading off in every
direction, but Allegra navigated them with
absolute certainty, the jangle of her

instrumented body telling the fairies which way to go.

Finally, the light grew brighter and the tunnel opened into a large, earthen room. After the near-silence of the catacombs, the sound here was almost deafening – a roaring cacophony of nearly every instrument imaginable, combined with shouts and roars of eager anticipation.

Allegra shuddered at the sound.

'It's The Game,' she explained in a disgusted voice. 'Everyone's excited to watch.'

She gestured to the end of the room, where wooden slats along one wall made a ladder that led to a small opening in the wall, like a window. The fairies exchanged glances and then flew up, pushing their faces together to share the view with Allegra, who climbed up the ladder to join them.

What they saw was a giant theatre, filled with what must have been nearly every resident of the Land of Music. They were all creatures like Allegra, each completely unique, with several musical instruments forming different parts of their bodies. In the mad din, tongue mallets played xylophone teeth, pick-shaped fingers plucked banjo bellies, and accordion heads squeezed air-horn noses.

Then suddenly it all stopped. There was silence . . . broken only by the sound of footsteps. The fairies looked up to the source of the sound – a plush box seat, directly over the curtained stage. Several uniformed creatures trooped in first – brutish-looking souls, many with harsh washboard chests, shrill whistle-noses and bodies of unstoppable brass. Finally, a woman strode in and the entire crowd gasped audibly.

'Queen Quadrille,' Allegra whispered.

The Queen carried herself with a gloriously regal air. Her bearing would have made her stand out in any crowd, but here she

was truly one of a kind. She was the only creature whose body was completely free of musical instruments. She made up for this in her clothing and accessories – jingle-bell earrings, a harmonica tiara and an exquisite form-fitted dress made of thousands of tiny, multicoloured finger cymbals, each etched with a perfect representation of Queen Quadrille's own stunning face.

'Can you see that?' whispered Silky eagerly.

What she was holding was a small, golden harp. Silky held up her crystal pendant and smiled, showing it to her friends. It was glowing bright red.

Before they could decide what to do next, the Queen spoke, and her voice echoed throughout the theatre.

'And now,' she cried, 'let The Game begin!'

Immediately the room burst into a wild roar of glee as every instrumented creature cried out in wild anticipation. Allegra shuddered and ducked away from the opening.

'I can't look,' she winced.

But the fairies couldn't take their eyes away from the stage. What made everyone react this way? What exactly was The Game?

Chapter Four

The Game

And then it began.

The curtain dropped, revealing two creatures on the stage, a man and a woman. They were both clearly nervous: the man's wood-block knees knocked together, punctuated by the woman's triangle ears, which tinkled against her mallet-ponytails as she shook. Both figures were rooted to the spot. Amazingly, the roar of the crowd grew even louder at the sight of these two poor creatures. It became so severe that Melody had to clap her hands over her sensitive ears.

Then Queen Quadrille stood up and majestically raised her arms.

'Do you see how the light reflects little rainbows off the cymbals?' Pinx whispered.

'Now imagine those on a dress. Can you picture it?'

Silky turned and looked at her disapprovingly.

'Too much?' Pinx asked.

Silky nodded silently.

Pinx thought for a moment, then said, 'You're right, maybe it's too much.'

They both resumed gazing at the Queen.

In the theatre, under the Queen's glare, the roar of the crowd died down to utter silence. Then the Queen turned her gaze to the two hapless creatures onstage. Her eyes settled on the woman.

'You,' the Queen intoned, 'may begin.'

The woman onstage cleared her throat. With a catch in her voice, she started to sing.

'We hail our Queen with boundless zeal, that gift of music Queen Quadrille . . .'

It was 'Hail to Queen Quadrille', the song all the plants had been singing.

'She's a little sharp,' Melody winced.

'Of course she is,' Allegra said from her spot at the bottom of the ladder. 'You'd be sharp too, if you were that frightened.'

Actually, Melody could never be sharp, but none of the fairies felt that this was the time to point it out.

'She really shouldn't be so nervous,' Melody noted. 'She has a lovely voice. And her violin technique is nearly perfect! Although I suppose when your arms are instruments it's hard not to get in your practice . . .'

As Melody thought about this, the woman finished, but no one applauded. It seemed as if no one even breathed. With nothing more than a whisper of shifting instruments, all eyes turned to the Queen, who in turn fixed her gaze on the man onstage.

'Now you,' the Queen boomed.

The pitifully nervous man warbled his way through his own version of 'Hail to Queen

Quadrille', singing several notes off key. Again, when he had finished, there was silence. All eyes turned to the Queen.

Melody shook her head.

'This is a terrible way to run a concert,' she tutted softly. 'No wonder they're both nervous – there's so much pressure! Where's the joy?'

'I don't think this is really a concert, Melody,' Petal said warily.

Like everyone else in the room, she was watching Queen Quadrille, who looked back and forth between the two singers, her shark-like eyes betraying no emotion.

'I don't understand,' whispered Bizzy. 'What's happening? What is she –'

But before she could finish her thought, Queen Quadrille settled her gaze on the female singer. The Queen extended her arm, her hand in a fist. She let it sit there for a moment and the entire room held its breath. Then she twisted her wrist upright and raised her thumb, giving the woman a thumbs-up sign.

Suddenly the theatre sprang back to life. With a wild din of toots, jingles and wails, the audience grew raucous again. The two performers, meanwhile, fell to their knees, the woman crying tears of relief as the man reached out desperately to the Queen.

'Please, Queen Quadrille, I beg of you –' he wailed.

But he got no further. The Queen fixed him with a wicked half smile, and turned her wrist over, thumbs down. With her other hand she forcefully pressed a button on the railing of her box, opening a trapdoor beneath the pleading man. A vacuum WHOOSH echoed through the theatre as the man was sucked down into its depths, still desperately pleading. As quickly as it had opened, the trapdoor slammed shut again, and wild shouts rose from the crowd.

Melody, Petal, Pinx, Silky and Bizzy could barely speak, they were so stunned by what they had just seen. Without realising it, they had all held on to each other for comfort, and now hovered in a close tangle. Together they turned to Allegra, who looked back sadly.

'What just happened to that man?' Silky asked. 'Is he . . .'

'He's trapped,' Allegra said. 'Sucked into a pit so soundless that he'll hear nothing – not even the sound of his own voice and instruments – for the rest of his life. That's The Game.'

'But that's horrible!' cried Melody.

'And that huge audience,' added Pinx incredulously, 'they *enjoy* this?'

Allegra shrugged, 'Partly they're just grateful it's not them . . . this time. And the other part –'

She was interrupted by the Queen's voice, which rose again, carrying over the discordant racket in the seats.

'Now, my people,' she cried, 'Who would like to hear some *real* music?'

'Cover your ears!' Allegra cried as the Queen began to play, but not fast enough.

Instantly, all five fairies were whisked into worlds of their own. Silky imagined herself riding on Misty, looping-the-loop through the stunning waterfalls of the Land of Endless Summer. Bizzy was in a giant kitchen, magically making millions of gingerbread men. Petal was back home with Uncle Delta in Fairyland, reading bedtime stories to sleepy farm animals. Pinx was strutting down the pink carpet at a Fairyland movie premiere. She posed for the cameras, enthralling the crush of reporters with her charm, quick wit and immaculate fashion sense.

As for Melody, the music crashed over her like a wave and curled around her like a blanket. There was nothing else for her but the song. Its perfect chords swirled around her, becoming a part of her. Melody was one with the music and she added her voice to its sound, her dance to its rhythm. Without realising it, she burst out through the opening and into the middle of the theatre itself, dancing and singing high above the centre of the stage.

Surprised by the sudden appearance of a fairy in her theatre, Queen Quadrille stopped playing the Harp, releasing everyone from its

mesmerising spell. With the jumbled sounds of
an orchestra tuning up, the instrument
creatures came back to themselves, as did
Melody's bewildered friends.

'Welcome back,' said Allegra.

'What happened?' Petal asked. 'I could have
sworn I was just back home ...'

'That was the harp,' Allegra explained. 'It's

another reason they listen to Queen Quadrille. When someone can give you your wildest dreams, it's hard to say no.'

'Um . . . I think we're missing someone,' Bizzy said, looking out of the opening.

'Melody!' Silky realised.

The girls pressed themselves to the opening, through which they could see a very confused-looking Melody hovering above the stage. All eyes in the theatre were fixed on her.

'So,' said Queen Quadrille, arching an eyebrow. 'We have a new songbird in our midst.'

'I remember music . . .' Melody said, trying to remind herself of where she was. 'Beautiful music . . .' She looked up at Queen Quadrille and beamed. 'It came from you!'

Melody flew up to the Queen's box, hovering just outside its rail, and bowed low.

'Your Highness,' she said, 'it is an honour to be in your presence.'

'*What*?' hissed Pinx from the hidden room. 'What is she doing?'

'It's the Land of Music,' Silky said, hopefully. 'Maybe Melody knows something we don't.'

'Let's hope so,' said Petal.

But the cries of the man sucked into the trapdoor still echoed ominously in their ears.

Chapter Five

Queen Quadrille

'Queen Quadrille,' Melody said formally, rising from her bow, 'as a fellow musician, I commend you on your playing.'

Queen Quadrille gave a slight nod.

'Thank you,' she replied. 'And as a fellow musician, I commend you on your voice and dance. They were . . . impressive.'

A flurry of squeaks, jingles and toots made the Queen turn back to her subjects, who were impatient now that the excitement was over.

'The Game is complete!' she declared. 'You may leave!'

This unleashed a riot of sound as all the Land's musical creatures rose to leave. Amid the tumult, the Queen beckoned Melody closer and leaned over to speak to her.

The other fairies strained to hear from their hiding place, but it was impossible. All they could see was faces – the Queen's stern and unmoving, Melody's furrowed and concentrating.

'What is she saying?' Bizzy asked nervously. 'Is Melody OK? Should we go and help her?'

Suddenly Melody threw back her head and laughed, as the Queen smiled and nodded.

'I think . . .' Silky began incredulously, 'the Queen just told her a joke.'

As the amazed fairies watched, Melody and the Queen exchanged what looked like more pleasantries, then Melody zoomed back down to their hiding spot, a grin on her face.

'Queen Quadrille has invited us for tea at the castle!' she exclaimed.

Pinx nearly toppled over in surprise.

'What?' she cried.

'Yes!' Melody replied in delight. 'I told her my friends and I wanted to talk to her about

* * * 53 * * *

her Harp, and she invited us for tea! Come on!'

Melody tried to flit out of the window, but Pinx quickly yanked her back.

'Hold it!' Pinx roared, and Melody turned to her, confused.

'What's wrong?' Melody asked.

'What's *wrong*?' Pinx exploded. 'When a Venomous Grubbluster Beast invites you to his lair for a snack, *you are the snack*!'

'I don't see what you're getting at,' said Melody, tilting her head.

'ARRRGH!' cried Pinx in frustration.

Silky stepped in to help her out.

'I think what Pinx means is that the Queen doesn't exactly seem ... trustworthy,' explained Silky.

Bizzy nodded.

'A get-together with the Ghastly Grand Guru of the Grisly Game?' she asked with a shudder. 'Gives me goosebumps.'

'It doesn't exactly seem like the wisest choice,' Petal agreed.

Melody shook her head, waving off their concerns.

'I know she can be cruel,' Melody agreed, 'but even an enchanted instrument doesn't play that beautifully for just anyone. There has to be good inside her. We just need to reach out to it. That'll change everything.'

There was something in Melody's tone, in the look in her eyes, and in her absolute faith that this was the right thing to do, that swayed them. After saying goodbye to Allegra, the five fairies slipped out of their hiding place and flew from the theatre. A guard with the body of a French horn and tambourine feet led them into a large, ivory carriage hitched to a team of beautiful harpsichord horses.

'Welcome!' cried Queen Quadrille as the fairies piled into the carriage. The inside was richly upholstered in pink, with deep fuchsia

cushions and a light-pink feathery trim, which was all Pinx needed to see. As the horses trotted off with 'Hail to Queen Quadrille' chirping from their keyboards, Pinx gossiped with the Queen about design. The Queen responded with stories that had them all laughing, and in no time they were all chatting like old friends. All their fears seemed to have melted away. Melody even felt comfortable enough to ask about the Conservatory, though she couldn't look directly at the Queen as she did.

'Conservatory?' the Queen asked.

'I would love to see it,' Melody said, and lowered her gaze to her lap as she struggled to sound casual. 'I mean, I know I didn't earn an invitation myself, but . . .'

'Oh, darling,' the Queen said, 'surely you're not doubting your talent? I've never heard a voice come close to yours. The lack of invitation was an oversight, nothing more.'

Melody practically glowed with happiness, and Silky could tell she wanted to talk more about the Conservatory, but they had already spent a lot of time in the Land of Music.

'Queen Quadrille,' Silky interjected, 'I know that Melody told you that we want to speak to you about your Harp . . .'

Silky quickly explained the Harp's true Talisman nature. She told the Queen about their mission, and why it was so important to take the Enchanted Harp back to the Faraway Tree right away, before Talon could steal it or the Land of Music moved on.

The Queen listened intently to the story and then slapped her hands down on her thighs. 'Done,' she proclaimed. 'The Enchanted Harp is yours.'

She held it out to Silky, but before the fairy could grab it, the Queen hugged it back to her chest with a mischievous smile.

'*After* you join me in the castle for a spot of

tea,' she added. 'I insist.'

Silky tried to protest, but the Queen would have none of it, and only clutched the Harp more tightly until the fairies relented.

The castle was surrounded by a high wall of solid rock. A gate in the wall stood open, awaiting the Queen's arrival. As her carriage pulled in, the fairies marvelled at the castle itself. It was a musical masterpiece. It was made of eight cylinders of various heights, which created an enormous pipe organ, majestically chiming the notes of 'Hail to Queen Quadrille' as the wind wafted through them. Inside, Queen Quadrille's song was whistled from teapots and hummed on the lips of ladies-in-waiting and courtiers. Even window washers' sponges seemed to squeak the song's melody as they rubbed against the glass panes. And when the group climbed the staircase to Queen Quadrille's private quarters, each piano-key step chimed out a note of the tune.

Finally, they reached a large room at the uppermost level of the castle, where Queen Quadrille paused just inside a large, gilded door.

'Melody,' the Queen beckoned. 'My castle has one more musical surprise for you.'

The Queen gestured to a thick, golden rope that hung from the ceiling.

'Come,' she urged, 'give it a pull.'

Silky thought that she could see a triumphant gleam in the Queen's eye, but before she could stop Melody, the Twinkletune Fairy stepped away from her friends to join the Queen. Then she reached up and pulled on the rope, making a steel door SLAM down.

On one side stood Melody and Queen Quadrille; Pinx, Silky, Petal and Bizzy were left on the other. Before Melody's shocked friends could even shout her name, a trapdoor opened at their feet and a vacuum WHOOSH

pulled them spiralling down, down, down into
a long, darkened chute.

Chapter Six

The Golden Cage

Queen Quadrille must have played the Enchanted Harp again; that was the only explanation. One minute Melody was watching in shock as a steel door separated her from her friends, the next minute she was whisked away on a cloud of song.

She came back to herself inside a large, golden cage, suspended from the ceiling and hanging not far off the ground. Melody jumped up to pull at the strong bars.

'AAAHHH!' she screamed, leaping back in shock as a fierce dog with the head of a trumpet sprang up to the cage, barking wildly as it bared its piercingly sharp brass teeth.

'Good morning,' Queen Quadrille cooed.

Melody turned to see the Queen sitting in

her note-shaped throne, right next to the cage.

'Welcome to my throne room,' the Queen continued. 'You should feel honoured – it's where I keep all my favourite possessions.'

Looking around, Melody could see that this was true. Pedestals all around the room were filled with tributes to Queen Quadrille's greatness: there were bejewelled busts, ivory and onyx music boxes, majestic portraits and row upon row of the finest musical instruments Melody had ever seen. For a moment these were so distracting that she almost forgot her situation.

'Is that a Mahogandary Bell?' she gasped.

There were only three of these in the entire Enchanted World, and their tone was so pure and magnificent that it had once reduced an army of stone golems to tears.

'It is,' the Queen replied. 'I own all the Enchanted World's most beautiful instruments . . . including you.'

'*Me?*' Melody said with a gasp. 'You think you own *me?*'

'Don't I?' said the Queen. 'If not, go ahead – hop on out.'

The Queen frowned in mock sympathy as Melody desperately rattled the cage bars.

'See?' she continued. 'You're mine. And the first thing we need to do is teach you 'Hail to Queen Quadrille', so you can perform it at the end of the next Game. It's a simple ditty, won't take you any time at all.'

'I would never sing that song, and I will never be a part of your awful Game!' Melody declared. 'What happened to you? Every other Queen Quadrille loved and celebrated music. They knew it was about freedom and happiness. But you –'

'Enough!' snapped Queen Quadrille. 'I have no interest in other queens. My interest is in you singing my song, which you'll do . . . or I'll destroy your precious Talisman. Or would you rather I give it to your friend, Talon? I'm sure he'll be around asking for it.'

'You wouldn't!' gasped Melody, 'the entire Enchanted World —'

'Is relying on you,' the Queen finished. 'I'll give you a little time to think about that.'

She waggled her fingers and glided off, leaving Melody yelling in frustration.

'You should be happy,' muttered a male voice behind her.

Melody turned to see a boy with the long, lean body of a bassoon.

'At least she's keeping you,' he continued. 'I got caught singing an unauthorised song. Now I have to play the next Game.'

'No,' declared Melody. 'I'm getting out of here, and I'll find a way to get you out, too. What's your name?'

'Bassilio,' said the boy.

'Distract the dog, Bassilio,' said Melody. I'm going to transform myself into water and spill out between the bars of this cage.'

'You can do that?' Bassilio asked.

'Yes,' said Melody simply. 'If I know an object well enough, I can transform into it. Now – the dog.'

Bassilio looked stumped – how was he supposed to distract the dog? He stuck a leg out from between the bars of the cage.

'Here, puppy,' he called. 'A nice, juicy leg, trying to escape.'

The dog saw Bassilio's leg waggling between the bars and pounced towards it, but Bassilio drew it back just in time. Next he dangled out an arm . . . another leg . . . the other arm . . . every time whisking it back into the cage mere seconds ahead of the dog's razor-teeth. But Bassilio was getting tired, and he wasn't sure he could keep it up for long.

'Are you out yet?' he turned and called.

Bassilio was shocked by what he saw. A large puddle was slowly rolling towards the edge of the cage. He was so mesmerised that he forgot the dog, who suddenly realised that the boy was now alone in the cage. In a flash, the dog started barking wildly, and Queen Quadrille stormed back into the room.

Rage twisted the Queen's face as she noticed the Melody-less cage.

'Where is she?' she growled.

Bassilio shrank back as far as he could go.

'I don't know,' he squeaked.

Suddenly the Queen noticed the puddle of water that was about to slip between the bars. Queen Quadrille quickly swept up the Mahogandary Bell, turning it upside-down and placing it at the edge of the raised cage, so the puddle would flow into it.

'Well then,' said the Queen smugly, 'if you don't know where Melody is, you won't mind if I give this to Otto. He is *so* thirsty.'

Holding the bell like a goblet, the Queen walked towards her panting dog, slowly lowering the water to his giant, thirsty tongue.

Chapter Seven

The Soundless Pit

Like Melody, the other four fairies lost track of time after the trapdoor opened and they were sucked away. Silky remembered being drawn deeper and deeper, twirling and swirling as she and the others plunged downwards. They tried to beat their wings and fly away, but it was no use. They were helpless.

The fairies were pulled into a small cavern where the suction stopped and they tumbled to the ground. The last thing Silky saw before her head hit the floor was a trapdoor in the ceiling slamming shut.

Silky wasn't sure when she regained consciousness, because the world was still pitch black and she couldn't hear a sound. Suddenly she felt a hand on her arm and flinched, then realised that it must be one of her friends. She squeezed the hand back gratefully.

Now for some light. Silky concentrated and used her power as an Illuminating Fairy to spread a gentle glow throughout the room. The first thing she saw was Bizzy, who was holding her hand.

'Hi,' Silky said.

At least she *thought* she said it, but she didn't hear a thing. She tried again.

Nothing. Bizzy shook her head and pointed to her own ears – she hadn't heard anything either. Now Silky understood. They were trapped in a soundless pit.

Silky looked around for the others and saw Petal leaning against a wall and smiling, clearly amused as she gazed at something above her head. Silky nudged Bizzy and pointed to Petal – what could be so funny? Then Petal noticed her friends watching, and nodded for them to follow her gaze.

Pinx was flapping against the ceiling in a silent rage. Her face grew redder and redder as she flitted from wall to wall, waving her arms and kicking her legs, shouting soundlessly at the top of her lungs. For a moment Silky, Petal and Bizzy were glad that the room was soundproof, because they couldn't even imagine the fit Pinx would have had if she could have heard them laughing at her.

Finally, Silky flew up to Pinx and put a hand on her friend's shoulder, trying to calm her down. She gestured for the others to follow, and they flew up to the trapdoor in the ceiling. All four of them pushed with every ounce of their energy, but it wouldn't budge. This sent Pinx into another silent rage, while the others flew back down to the floor to consider their next step.

Suddenly Bizzy perked up, inspired. She grabbed Petal and Silky's arms excitedly, pointed to herself and then made a show of waggling her fingers then opening them with a flourishy POOF! They understood immediately – Bizzy could free them with a spell! They nodded encouragingly and then stepped back to give her some space.

Bizzy started to prepare. She shook out her hands. She rolled her neck: first one way and then the other. She took off her headband, shook out her hair and put the headband back on. She entwined her fingers and stretched her arms up to the ceiling . . . to the right . . . to the left . . .

She took a deep breath. She took another. Finally, she closed her eyes and moved her lips, silently speaking her spell and concentrating for all she was worth.

Nothing. Not even a Basic Bizzy Blunder, like 'soap and boars' instead of an 'open door'. Nothing.

Although Bizzy was a Conjurer Fairy, she was still just a Spell-Caster-in-Training. She was not strong enough to cast spells without saying them out loud.

Bizzy was visibly crushed, and although her friends put their arms around her and nodded that it was OK, they were all clearly worried. How were they ever going to get out?

With no other options, Bizzy, Silky and Pinx did the only thing they could do. They flew to the trapdoor, banged madly on it with their fists and feet and screamed for help at the top of their lungs. It was useless, of course, because their voices and banging were

swallowed by the perfect soundproofing. They
may as well have been pounding pillows and
screaming in outer space. Even so, the effort
completely exhausted them, and after several
minutes even Pinx felt completely empty. Their
shoulders slumped and their eyelids drooped as
they sank back down to the floor and leaned
against each other, defeated and devastated.

Only Petal remained upright. She stood
perfectly still in the middle of the room with
her eyes shut. Silky was the first to notice, and

when she did she nudged Pinx and Bizzy, who started watching Petal too. At first glance, Petal looked completely relaxed, but when her friends looked closely enough, they could see a tiny muscle twitching in her forehead. It was the faintest movement, just enough to show that she was concentrating very hard – excruciatingly hard.

Petal remained like that for several minutes, then Bizzy grabbed Pinx and Silky's arms excitedly and pointed at the floor. Like the tip of a drill bit, a thick vine was twisting its way up from underground, loosening the soil as it pushed its way into the room. At first it was just a shoot, but it quickly grew taller . . . and taller . . . and taller . . .

Still concentrating, Petal opened her eyes and nodded to her friends. Petal took hold of the vine, and Silky, Pinx and Bizzy did the same. They rose with the vine as it sped all the way up to the earthen ceiling. Petal locked

eyes with her friends, trying to communicate
what would happen next. This was their only
hope. They all took the deepest breath possible,
shut their eyes tightly and clung to the vine
with all their might as it drilled through the
ceiling, pushing through layer after layer of
dirt, straining to move quickly enough to get
them up to the surface before they ran out of
breath.

The vine burst through the earth into the

beautiful dusklight just outside the castle walls. The four fairies gasped, collapsing into the tall grass and gratefully filling their lungs with fresh air.

Then they started to laugh.

'We're free!' Silky cried.

'Fabulously, Fantastically, *Finally* Free!' Bizzy added.

'AAAHHH!' Pinx squealed, ecstatic just to hear the sound of her own voice.

'Petal, you did it!' Silky exclaimed.

But when she turned to look at Petal, she realised that her friend wasn't well at all. Petal was still lying in the spot where she'd rolled off the vine, and although she offered Silky a wan smile, she couldn't move or even speak.

'Is she OK?' Bizzy asked.

Silky couldn't answer. She didn't know.

'She did it to save us, even though it was too much for her,' Pinx whispered, 'and now she's going to –'

'Stop!' Silky demanded. 'She's going to be *fine*.'

'Silky! Bizzy! Pinx! Petal!'

The fairies spun around at the sound of their names and saw a familiar figure racing towards them from the bushes.

'Allegra!' Silky shouted as the girl ran, her wind-chime hair singing out every step.

'I'm so glad you're OK!' cried Allegra. 'I was so worried when you went off with Queen Quadrille. I've been watching the castle just to make sure.'

Allegra's expression changed as she saw Petal.

'What happened?' she asked. 'And where's Melody?'

Silky, Pinx and Bizzy explained it all, jumping in on each other as they shared all the details.

'. . . so we have to get back inside the castle right away,' Silky finished. 'Melody's in there somewhere, and she's with Queen Quadrille!'

Allegra shook her head.

'I can get you into the castle, and I can help you find Melody, but not now,' she said.

'What's wrong with now?' demanded Pinx.

Before Allegra could answer, the girls heard something ear-splittingly loud whizzing through the air, growing louder and louder as it drew closer. They looked up and their eyes grew wide. It was *Talon*.

The Troll was a vision of evil. His stooped figure stood on a bewitched cymbal plant, and his black robes flapped around him as he scanned the area from left to right.

'Get down!' Silky cried.

They all fell into the tall grass, seeking whatever cover they could find as Talon zoomed overhead, looking . . . looking . . . He soared so close that they could hear his putrid panting as it rasped from his throat. The girls held their breath. Would he see them?

He didn't spot them. He flew off, still
scanning the Land of Music for the Talisman
he craved. The fairies sighed in relief.

'That's Talon,' Silky explained. 'He's after
the Enchanted Harp too, which means it's
even more important that we get inside and
rescue Melody and the Harp *now*.'

'We can't,' Allegra said. 'The gate's closed for the night; we can't get in.'

'So we'll fly over the gate!' Silky insisted.

'I can't fly,' Allegra retorted. 'And without my help, you could get lost and trapped again.'

'And look at Petal,' Bizzy added. 'She can't fly anywhere tonight. Maybe we should just wait until morning.'

Petal was curled up in the grass, fast asleep. Much as Silky hated to admit it, her friend was right. Petal needed to rest, and it wouldn't be wise to split up or navigate the castle without Allegra. Silky took a deep breath.

'OK,' she said. 'We'll wait until morning.'

Bizzy, Pinx and Silky carried Petal between them as Allegra led the group to the Countermeasures' catacombs, the closest place to sleep for the night. But Silky couldn't rest. She was too tortured by the questions that kept running through her head. What if they couldn't find Melody? What if Petal couldn't recover? What if they woke up and Talon had already found the Harp? What if the Land of Music moved away from the Faraway Tree?

It was going to be a long night.

Chapter Eight

Melody or the Harp

Queen Quadrille grinned as Otto's thirsty tongue moved ever closer to the water in the Mahogandary Bell.

'Drink up, Otto boy,' the Queen cooed. 'After all,' she added, with a meaningful glance at the boy in the cage, 'it's just water!'

Bassilio winced and turned away – he couldn't bear to see Melody lapped up by the watchdog. But just as Otto's greedy tongue was about to make contact, Melody turned back into herself. Far too big for the Mahogandary Bell now, she toppled on to the floor.

'Hold her, Otto,' ordered Queen Quadrille.

The massive trumpet-dog promptly sat on Melody's midriff, knocking the wind out of

her and pinning her securely to the floor.

Queen Quadrille leaned down to look Melody in the eye. Then she gave a mirthless smile.

'You're very crafty, my pet,' she cooed. 'I see now that I'll have to discipline you.'

Melody tried not to let the Queen see how nervous she felt. What would happen to her?

The Queen removed the golden cage and replaced it with a thick glass box, into which she deposited both Melody and Bassilio.

'Comfy?' asked the Queen, as soon as her captives were sealed securely inside. 'I hope so, because you will be there for a very long time. It's my own invention – made from glass that won't shatter even at the highest musical note ever sung by a living creature. Sweet dreams, my songbird.'

She breezed out of the room and Melody stared after her, a bewildered look on her face.

'Melody?' said Bassilio.

Melody just shook her head, lost in thought.

'A box made to trap songs,' she mused. 'A real music lover would never even think of something like that. And she's a Queen Quadrille . . .'

'Melody?' Bassilio tried again, this time resting a hand on her shoulder. 'I have an idea to get us out of here.'

This caught Melody's attention and she whirled to face the boy.

'How?' she asked.

'You could transform into a diamond!' he said. 'Diamonds cut glass!'

'Yes!' Melody squealed. 'A diamond! I can become a diamond!'

She hugged Bassilio's tiny bassoon body and lifted him off the floor . . . but then a cloud crossed her face and she let him go.

'I don't know how to become a diamond,' she said, sadly. 'I don't think I've even seen a real one, just pictures. And if I don't know something well . . .'

'Can you try?' Bassilio asked.

The look in his eyes was so hopeful that Melody's heart ached for him.

'I'll try,' she said.

Bassilio backed away to give her room, and Melody concentrated as hard as she could on every image she had ever seen of a diamond. Within seconds she had disappeared . . . and in her place was a large gem. It was the most beautiful, perfectly formed diamond Bassilio had ever seen.

'Yes!' he cried ecstatically.

He snatched it up and ran it against the glass wall.

Nothing.

He tried it again.

Not even a scratch.

Frustrated and anxious, Bassilio scraped the diamond along the glass wall, faster and harder, again and again and again ... until Melody appeared in his arms, clutching her forehead.

'Ohhhh, my head,' she groaned. 'Bassilio, you have to stop.'

'Sorry,' Bassilio winced, 'I just kept hoping ...'

'I know,' Melody said softly. 'Me too. I just didn't know diamonds well enough.'

Disappointed, but with no other ideas, the two settled into a fitful and uneasy sleep.

They were awakened in the first light of morning by a flurry of creaks, scratches and footsteps. They jumped to their feet. Outside the cage, they could see Otto the dog still curled up, fast asleep, but someone was definitely coming.

'The guards?' Bassilio asked quietly.

Melody nodded, adding, 'Or the Queen.'

They stood back against the far glass wall of their cage, warily awaiting whatever happened next.

THUMP!

'Ow!' said a familiar voice. 'I swear, if I'd seen this room I would never have trusted Queen Quadrille. Who decorates like this? I can't even move without tripping!'

'Pinx?' Melody cried.

She ran to the edge of her box and spotted them: Pinx, Bizzy, Petal and Silky. Melody had never been so happy to see anyone in her life.

'Pinx!' she shouted. 'Over here!'

'Melody!' the fairies screamed back.

Bassilio tried to quieten them but his

warning came too late. Otto sprang up, barking and growling, and lunged for the girls, his razor-teeth bared and ready to bite.

At the last possible second, Pinx pulled off her scarf and flung it over Otto's trumpet mouth, quickly tying it into a knot.

'There,' said Pinx, watching the whining dog paw at his mouth. '*This* is why it's important to accessorise.'

Everyone giggled except Petal. She was sitting between Silky and Bizzy and she didn't

even smile, but just lowered her head.

'Oh, Petal, please don't be upset,' Melody asked. 'He really isn't the nicest dog.'

'Petal isn't upset, Melody,' Bizzy said.

Melody realised that Petal wasn't sitting because she disapproved, but because she was unable to support her own weight.

'What happened?' Melody gasped.

Petal heard the fear in Melody's voice. She summoned the strength to smile and slowly croak, 'I'll be . . . fine. Just need rest and . . . dragon-tear tea . . .'

'Which we can get from Dido,' Silky added, looking at Melody. 'Right after we free you and get the Harp. Stand back.'

Melody joined Bassilio at the far end of the box, and watched as Silky concentrated her light into a powerful laser beam, which she shot at the glass prison, slicing away a perfectly circular hole. Melody and Bassilio scrambled out in relief.

'Thank you,' gushed Bassilio to Silky, then he turned to Melody. 'Thank you.'

'You're welcome,' Melody smiled. 'Now go – get as far away as you can.'

With a final grin of thanks, Bassilio ran out of the room, leaving the five fairies to jump into each other's arms for a huge hug.

'I'm so glad you found me!' cried Melody. 'How did you get past the Queen?'

'You think it was easy?' Pinx asked.

She, Silky and Bizzy started excitedly talking over each other as they explained how Allegra had smuggled them into the castle when the gates opened, past all the guards. From there the fairies had remembered the way to the throne room, where Bizzy did a spell to open the door.

'You did?' Melody interjected, thrilled that one of Bizzy's spells had worked so perfectly.

'Sort of,' Bizzy admitted. 'My spell was supposed to get the door open, but it actually got the door *mopin'* . . .'

'Which was perfect,' said Silky with a grin, 'because the door climbed off its hinges and went to sulk in a corner – look!'

She pointed to where the door had indeed slunk into a corner. It was hunched over, sighing heavily.

'But Melody, we saw Talon,' continued Silky.

'Talon?' Melody gasped.

'So we need to move quickly,' Silky continued. 'We need the Harp, which means we need to find Queen Quadrille. Do you know where she is?'

'Why, I'm right behind you, darling,' rang out the familiar voice.

The fairies spun around to see Queen Quadrille in the doorway. As always, the Harp was in her hands, although it now sat in a thick-walled, transparent box.

Silky stepped forwards, a commanding look

on her face, and stared the Queen in the eye.

'I suggest you honour your promise and give us the Harp,' she demanded. 'We'll fight you for it if we have to, and with five of us and only one of you, your chances don't look good.'

'Hmm, excellent point,' said the Queen.

She placed two fingers in her mouth and whistled. Immediately, a seemingly endless troop of brass instrument guards marched into the room, filling the space behind Queen Quadrille and glaring at the fairies with angry eyes.

'I like these odds better,' oozed the Queen. 'But still, fights can get so messy, and you say you *are* trying to save the Enchanted World, so I'd like to make you an offer. I will give you the Harp and you will give me Melody. It's not quite an even trade, since I get the finer of the two instruments, but . . .'

'Trade Melody for the Harp?' Silky

repeated, her eyes wide with disbelief.

Pinx pushed to the front of the group.

'Are you insane?' she shouted at the Queen.

'That's Riotously Ridiculous Rot!' Bizzy agreed.

Even Petal managed to shake her head.

Then Melody stepped forwards.

'It's a deal,' she said simply.

'What?'

'What are you saying?'

'Are you mad?'

A wild chorus of protests from her friends rained down on Melody, but she ignored them. She turned to Silky and spoke with absolute calm and certainty.

'Time's running out,' she said. 'Talon's here. The Ladder could move at any time. You have to go.'

Silky locked eyes with Melody and was struck again by what she had first noticed back at home. Melody seemed to be soft and gentle, and she was, but deep inside her was a core of steel. Anyone who underestimated that was in for trouble.

'Are you sure?' Silky asked.

This triggered another hail of protests from Bizzy, Pinx and Petal, but Silky and Melody didn't even hear them. Melody just nodded, smiling gently.

'Let me go,' she said, and in her head Silky could hear what Melody had said back in their treehouse: 'I can do anything I set my mind to.'

Silky smiled back at her friend and then turned to the Queen.

'You heard Melody,' she said. 'It's a deal.'

'Perfect,' replied the Queen.

She held out the Harp to Silky, who saw that its box was going to be almost impossible to open. They could do it, but it would take time – more time than they'd have in the Land of Music.

'Insurance,' the Queen said. 'So you don't use its enchanting powers while you're here.'

Silky took the Harp, and the Queen immediately signalled to her guards, who swarmed around Melody, pulling her away from Petal, Bizzy and Pinx.

'We should go,' Silky said to her friends.

Although it hurt her heart to do it, she turned away from Melody and flew out. Bizzy and Pinx reluctantly followed her, holding Petal between them.

'I hope Melody knows what she's doing,' Pinx muttered as they soared out of the castle.

'Me too,' Silky said, working hard to banish every doubt from her mind. 'Me too.'

Chapter Nine

Talon's Return

At first it was the hardest thing in the universe, flying off to the Ladder without Melody. Silky, Petal, Bizzy and Pinx moved slowly, each of them hoping against hope that they would soon hear Melody behind them, racing to catch up.

'This is madness,' said Silky finally. 'Melody stayed behind to save the Harp. If we don't fly at full speed and get it back to the Tree, her sacrifice was for nothing. Do we want that?'

None of them wanted it, of course. Bizarre as it seemed, the best way to show their love for Melody was to leave her behind, and trust that she would somehow find her way home.

Newly determined, the group zoomed back over the Land of Music, whizzing past fields of flutes, over mountains made of titanic bass drums and through great guitar gorges, until finally they saw it – the spot where they had emerged into the Land.

'Right there!' Silky cried, pointing out to the horizon.

But before the fairies could even get halfway to the Ladder, a loud WHOOSH rang through the marsh. A figure zoomed in front of them, stopping them in their tracks, and the wind stirred up in its wake aroused a wail from the harmonicas, recorders and didgeridoos. The figure flew back seconds later, this time stopping to hover in front of the fairies and reveal his identity. It was Talon.

He stood in front of the fairies on his flying cymbal, towering over and leering down at them. His crooked nose seemed to point to the stolen crystal around his neck, the source of all his power. His sallow skin stood out against the black of his robes, and his yellow teeth

made his cruel smile gruesome.

Silky, Pinx and Bizzy considered making a run for it, but they had learned that tackling Talon without a plan could be disastrous. With Petal unwell, it seemed wiser to bide their time and wait for the opportunity to make their move.

'So,' sneered Talon, his rancid breath wafting down to the fairies and enveloping them in its stench, 'we meet again. I saw you last night, you know, in the fields outside the castle. I knew that if I just waited, you'd do all the work and get the Enchanted Harp for me, which you did. You are so predictable.'

Talon leaned forwards on his flying cymbal and the magic disc carried him slowly towards Silky.

Pinx and Bizzy looked at each other. Petal was between them, one of her arms draped over each of their shoulders. Silky needed them, but there was no way either of them could carry Petal alone, and Petal was in no shape to fly by herself. What should they do?

'Hurry!' Silky cried, as she lost more ground to Talon.

'Drop me,' Petal whispered. 'Do it.'

Bizzy and Pinx looked down at Petal and then over at Silky, who was edging away from Talon. They winced, and then released Petal and flew to Silky's side.

Petal had no strength to fly. She fell down, down, down towards the marsh. As she fell, she whispered a cry for help to the plants and animals. A grand pianofern swayed into her path and caught her gently on its keys, which cradled her like a hammock.

Talon knew that he needed to distract the three feisty fairies, so he turned his attention to Petal, their weak link. With a wicked grin, he plucked a recorder from the ground and muttered a spell. With a shrill whistle, the instrument shot out of the Troll's hand, aiming

straight for Petal.

However, the gongs had also heard Petal's plea, and one of them leaned into the path of the spell to protect her. The recorder bounced off the gong's shiny brass, darting harmlessly into the distance.

Talon and the fairies were stuck. As long as Pinx, Bizzy and Silky kept the box, Talon couldn't get to it; and Talon couldn't seem to deflect their attention elsewhere. Unless . . .

Talon tilted his head, listening. He sniffed the air. He licked a finger and raised it, calculating the direction of the wind. Then he turned to Silky, Bizzy and Pinx.

'It's the Land,' he declared with a nasty smile. 'I can feel it starting to move away from the Ladder. *I* can get back home even without the Ladder. Can you? If not, you'll want to release the Harp and make a run for it before you and your injured friend are trapped here forever.'

'You're bluffing!' cried Pinx, but there was fear in her eyes.

'What if he's not bluffing?' Bizzy whispered anxiously. 'We can't get home without the Ladder, and if we're stuck here forever, Petal won't get dragon-tear tea. She'll never get better!'

Silky looked at Petal, who was still cradled in the grand pianofern. Was Talon telling the truth? Melody had already put herself in danger for them. By staying and fighting, would they be sacrificing Petal too?

Chapter Ten

Melody Plays The Game

Once again, the theatre in the Land of
Music was filled to bursting with
instrument creatures of all shapes and sizes.
Every one of them was cheering, drumming,
whistling or tooting their excitement at
witnessing another Game. As always, the
sound died away as Queen Quadrille
appeared in her theatre box.

'Today, my subjects, I have a special treat
for you, a change in The Game,' the Queen
announced. 'From now on, contestants won't
challenge a fellow subject from the Land of
Music. They'll take on the most glorious
songbird the Enchanted World can offer: my
new pet, Melody!'

The crowd exploded in a riot of musical

tones as the curtain dropped to reveal Melody, trapped in a solid glass box that sat on one of the stage's trapdoors. The box was made of the same material as the one Silky had ruined; it was shatterproof to the highest musical note ever sung by a living creature.

Despite the roar of the crowd, Melody looked unmoved. The Queen leaned forwards and delivered her next speech directly to the fairy, eager to see her reaction.

'And for your opponent,' lilted the Queen, 'I've brought a face from your past.'

There was a loud jangle of drums, whistles and chimes as several brass-bodied guards dragged Allegra on to the stage, forcing her to stand on the other trapdoor.

'Allegra!' cried Melody.

'They caught me,' Allegra explained sadly, 'after I helped the others to sneak inside the castle.'

Thrilled by Melody's distress, the Queen

decided to rub salt in her wounds, gleefully going over the rules that everyone in the audience already knew.

'At my signal, each contestant will sing my beautiful anthem,' she declared. 'When they have finished, I will sentence the worst one to an eternity in my soundless pit!'

This thrilled the audience, and their jangling glee echoed through the theatre as Melody and Allegra quickly tried to speak.

'You'll win,' said Allegra. 'No one can sing better than you.'

'Don't be ridiculous,' Melody retorted. 'I'll throw it; I'll sing off-key.'

But Allegra just smiled wanly. She had heard Melody's voice. She doubted that it could ever sound off-key, no matter how hard Melody tried. She was right, of course. The few times Melody had attempted to make a joke and sing off-key, she had only succeeded in changing the song into a minor key that sounded even more glorious than the original.

Unwilling to give up, Melody shouted to the Queen as the crowd noise slowed, 'I won't play your Game, Queen Quadrille! I refuse to sing!'

The Queen's smile only broadened; she had expected this.

'If you refuse, you'll both lose, and plunge down to separate pits,' she said, leaning forwards and relishing the agonising choice. 'You can't save your little friend, Melody. Shouldn't you at least try to save yourself?'

Melody had no idea how to respond – what could she do? Allegra understood her distress.

'It's OK,' she reassured Melody.

Although her voice and words were strong, Allegra's wind-chime hair gave her away – it tinkled as she trembled in fear.

'No,' Melody said, shaking her head. 'There has to be another way . . .'

Suddenly a calm seemed to spread over Melody. She smiled at the Queen.

'You're right,' she called to her captor. 'I should at least try. I'm ready.'

'Excellent,' beamed the Queen. 'Begin.'

The room fell into utter silence as Melody began to sing.

'We hail our Queen with boundless zeal, that gift of music Queen Quadrille . . .'

Her voice rang out with perfect pitch and tone, and every instrument creature in the room grew silent, completely captivated by the spell of Melody's gorgeous voice. It was easily the loveliest version of 'Hail to Queen Quadrille' anyone had ever heard, and when Melody reached the final note, she added a flair of her own, allowing her voice to flow higher and higher along the musical scale.

And higher and higher.

And higher . . . and higher . . .

Melody didn't stop. She didn't take a breath.

She let her voice soar further and further into the farthest reaches of the high notes, and even Queen Quadrille was mesmerised. She listened breathlessly as Melody hit notes no one had ever heard before, her alabaster face turning pink, then a stunning red as she climbed still higher . . . and higher . . . and higher . . .

With an ear-piercing CRACK! the glass around Melody shattered and fell to the ground.

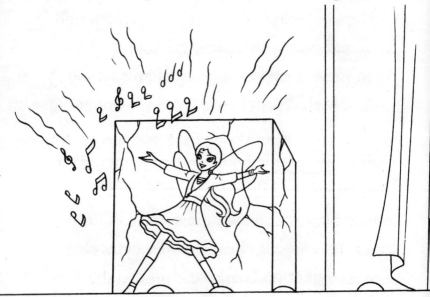

Melody spread her wings and rose into the air, flying up to Queen Quadrille.

'But that's impossible!' Queen Quadrille cried. 'That glass was shatterproof!'

'Shatterproof to the highest note ever sung by a living creature,' Melody reminded her. 'That creature was my great-great-grandmother Soprana.'

The Queen gasped as Melody shrugged, smiling playfully.

'So I had to sing higher,' she said.

The crowd roared, entranced by Melody's musical prowess. Melody couldn't help but giggle as she rewarded them with a bow – she hadn't been sure that she could actually do it.

But while Melody acknowledged the crowd, she forgot to pay attention to Queen Quadrille, who was livid that her plans had been spoiled. With a snarl she pressed the button in her box seat that opened Allegra's trapdoor.

Allegra screamed as she began to fall, but Melody swooped and caught her just before the girl could be sucked into the depths.

'Get her!' screeched the Queen to her swarm of guards onstage, but they just stared at each other. After watching Melody sing the impossible, they were very much in awe of her, and far too intimidated to make a move.

Their hesitation was all Melody needed. She flew back to Queen Quadrille, staring her in the eye. Melody saw only venom there, and all the questions that had plagued Melody since she heard about this Queen bubbled to the surface again. The guards, the audience and everything else around them melted away as Melody faced Queen Quadrille.

'Help me to understand,' Melody implored the Queen. 'How can a Queen Quadrille do all this? Great music comes from *happiness*. No one should know that better than you, you're from the most musical family in history . . .'

That was when it dawned on Melody: what was the one thing that could drive a Queen Quadrille to destroy the very thing that her entire family, generation after generation, valued most? Melody's jaw dropped.

'You have no ear for music!' she realised.

Melody was concentrating so hard on the Queen that she had forgotten they weren't alone. She was actually surprised when she heard the collective harmonic gasp from the audience. In the Land of Music, this was the most terrible charge imaginable. The Queen was quick to deny it.

'That's preposterous!' she huffed, and turned to address everyone in the crowd. 'You've all heard me play the Harp! Have you ever heard another instrument so beautiful?'

'The Harp is enchanted,' Melody replied gently. 'Can you play anything else?'

Melody turned to the crowd.

'Please, does anyone here have an instrument the Queen can play?' she asked.

Several of the guards in the box with the Queen held out instruments for her, but the Queen brushed them away.

'I don't play my subjects' instruments,' she sneered.

'OK,' Melody said mildly, 'then sing with me.'

Melody began a simple, beautiful tune.

'This is preposterous!' the Queen blustered. 'I'm the Queen! I shouldn't have to . . .'

But her voice trailed away. Every creature in the theatre was staring at her, and suspicion had filled their eyes. If the Queen was going to have even the slightest chance of maintaining her hold on her subjects, there was only one thing she could do. She took a deep breath and joined Melody for just a few notes . . . warbling horribly off-key.

A discordant roar shook the theatre, as

everyone realised that Melody had spoken the truth – Queen Quadrille had no ear for music!

'It must have been horrible for you,' Melody said. 'You were in line to be Queen Quadrille, the Enchanted World's greatest expert on music . . . and you're tone deaf. You must have been so ashamed, dreading the day your secret would come out, but then you found the Enchanted Harp and you knew it wouldn't have to. You played for the old Queen Quadrille – did you trap her somewhere while she dreamed? When you took over, you punished everyone in the Land of Music for having what you lacked.'

Now that Melody understood, she felt nothing but pity for Queen Quadrille, but pity was the last thing the Queen wanted. Her face contorted in fury as Melody spoke, and by the time the fairy had finished, the Queen could no longer contain her rage. She screamed and

leaped from her box, lunging for Melody.

The Queen landed on the fairy, and her
momentum sent them both falling backwards
through the air. It happened so quickly that
Melody had no time to get her bearings, and
her wings hung uselessly down her back. The
two looked like a single beast as they wrestled
in the air, falling down, down, down, until . . .

WHOOSH!

There was a horrified gasp from everyone

in the theatre as the Queen and Melody were sucked into the still-open trapdoor, and disappeared from sight. Immediately, the trapdoor slammed shut, and the Queen's screams faded into utter silence.

Chapter Eleven

Rise of the Queen

Despite the risks, Silky, Bizzy and Pinx couldn't let Talon have the Harp. The entire Enchanted World was relying on them, and any worries they had about getting stuck in the Land of Music, about Petal getting her tea or about Melody's capture had to come second. So the stand-off continued.

Talon plucked another recorder and muttered in Trollish. His crystal flashed, sending the instrument like an arrow towards the fairies. They dived to one side, crashing into a large gong. Dazed, the three fairies and the box fell with a thump, and lay on the ground. Talon allowed himself a moment to giggle before zooming down on his flying cymbal, reaching out for the box . . .

'No!' cried Silky, regaining her senses just as Talon's fingers brushed the Enchanted Harp's box. Immediately, she grabbed the box and darted up among the trees.

'I'm getting tired of this!' roared Talon, and muttered a Trollish spell.

His roar instantly revived Pinx and Bizzy, just in time to see six enchanted recorder reeds hurl themselves at Silky like spears.

'Look out, Silky!' they exclaimed.

Silky turned and her eyes grew wide with horror. There was no way she could avoid them all while holding the bulky Harp box.

'Bizzy!' Silky cried desperately. 'Take it!'

She dropped the box and then ducked, bobbed and weaved away from the spears, several of which impaled themselves in the tree where Silky had been just seconds before.

Bizzy swooped and caught the Harp box, but soon had to get rid of it when Talon enchanted several large hunks of harmonica

moss and sent them singing through the air towards her. Bizzy tossed the box to Pinx, and so it continued: the three fairies playing a deadly serious game of catch as Talon tried to stop them with every object he could find to throw. But Talon's missiles were becoming harder and harder to avoid, and it was only a matter of time before he hit the fairies and claimed the Harp as his own.

'I know what we need!' Bizzy suddenly cried, ducking out of the way as a flying grand pianofern whizzed overhead. 'Giants! A team of giants! They could carry us to the Ladder in a single step!'

'If the Ladder's even there!' Pinx retorted.

'Don't fight about it, just do it!' Silky yelled, contorting herself wildly to avoid a flurry of flying flute-trees.

Bizzy took a deep breath and concentrated, then cried, 'Geeno-gihno-whomper-stomper-blizz-bang!'

A shadow fell over the marsh.

'It's the giants!' cried Bizzy, elated. 'I did it!'

Then the shadow started to buzz, and Bizzy realised that she hadn't done it at all.

'Those aren't giants,' Pinx howled. 'Those are . . .'

'*Gnats!*' Silky screamed.

A massive swarm of gnats descended on the marsh. There were millions of them, and they flew in such thick swarms that nobody could see a thing, including Talon. Flying was no longer possible – the fairies couldn't see where

they were going. Instead, they all descended to the marshy ground, staggering back and forth as they swatted madly at the tiny black insects that took up their whole field of vision.

Then a voice rang out in the blackness, just audible above the buzzing. It was Pinx.

'Silky, Bizzy, the Harp!' she shouted. 'I lost the Harp!'

'What do you mean, you lost it?' Silky's voice shot back.

'I tripped! It fell out of my hands!'

'Pinx!' Silky rebuked.

'I couldn't help it!' Pinx retorted, 'I'd like to see *you* keep hold of a great big box when you're covered with creepy-crawlies.'

'I have it!' came a gleeful roar.

'*Talon*?' cried Silky and Pinx in despair.

'I've got it!' shouted Bizzy.

She had been racking her brain for the counterspell ever since the gnats arrived. Now she shouted it out to the skies.

'Nobus-stangous-allbegonah-buzzerous!'
she cried.

As quickly as they had come, the gnats
disappeared, and everyone could see again.
Silky, Bizzy and Pinx were on separate patches
of marsh grass. Talon lay still in the boggy
waters of the marsh, his arms outstretched and
his mouth spread wide in a grin.

'Say goodbye to your Talisman, fairies,' he
said, spitting out the word 'fairies' as if it were
a curse. 'The Enchanted Harp is mine, all
mine!'

Triumphantly, he stood up, hoisting the box
in his hands high over his head.

Silky, Bizzy and Pinx burst out laughing.
Confused, Talon lowered the box to eye level.
While it was the size and shape of the Harp
box, it was actually a glockenspiel fish, and it
was not happy to be hoisted out of the water.
It spat a stream of smelly water into Talon's
face, and the Troll threw it back into the

marsh. Everyone's eyes followed the fish as it splashed down next to . . .

'The Harp!' everyone shouted.

They all raced for it at once, but it was someone else's hand that grabbed it first. Silky, Bizzy, Pinx and Talon looked up in surprise. Who could it be?

It was Queen Quadrille. She stood haughtily on a patch of marsh grass, the Harp in her hands, and stared at them all.

'Not another step closer, any of you,' she said. 'If you even think of using magic on me, I'll destroy the Harp immediately. I made the box; I can demolish it easily.'

Talon and the fairies froze. The Queen smiled.

'That's better,' she said. 'Now –'

'Where's Melody?' Silky interrupted.

Queen Quadrille turned on her. 'Melody is unimportant,' she declared. 'I want to talk about the Harp. I want to know which one of you wants it the most, and more importantly, what you will give me for it?'

'You must be joking!' Pinx exploded. 'We want the Harp to save the Enchanted World and Talon wants to destroy it – isn't that good enough for you?'

Talon gave a chortle, shaking his head.

'Your Majesty,' he oozed, bowing to Queen Quadrille. 'Don't listen to these fairies. They are, as you say, unimportant. I have no desire to destroy the Enchanted World. I want to *reimagine* it in my own image.'

He smiled, apparently trying to show that image to its best advantage. Silky, Pinx and Bizzy tried hard not to be sick.

'But I ask you, Your Majesty, what good is a universe in your own image without someone to share it?' Talon went on. 'Someone brilliant and beautiful ... someone like you.'

Talon slowly strode forwards as he spoke, until he was next to the Queen. She didn't object. He took her hand and kissed it. The Queen smiled. The fairies' mouths fell open.

'Wow,' Silky gaped.

'Is he *flirting* with her?' Pinx said in disgust. 'He's actually *flirting* with her!'

'That is the Gutwrenchingly Grossest Gush I have ever seen in my life,' marvelled Bizzy.

Talon removed his lips from the Queen's hand. 'I assure you, Your Majesty,' he said in an oily voice. 'If you give me the Harp, you will rule the Enchanted World by my side.'

'That is tempting,' replied the Queen, 'but I'd also like something more immediate.'

'Anything, Your Majesty,' said Talon.

'Good,' said the Queen, 'because I'm worried about one of the giant didgeridoos growing here in the marsh. It sounds clogged.'

'Clogged?' asked Talon, confused.

'Yes, clogged,' said the Queen. 'If you really want the Harp, you'll climb inside and remove anything that might be stuck. That, more than anything, would sway me.'

'What?' Pinx exclaimed, throwing her arms up in frustration. 'Honestly, if *that's* all you want, *I'll* –'

'Shhh,' Silky silenced her.

Silky was fairly certain she knew what was going on, and a smile played across her lips.

Talon rose from his knees and bowed to Queen Quadrille.

'If you want the didgeridoo unclogged, that's what you shall have, Your Majesty.'

'Thank you, Talon,' said Queen Quadrille.

She pointed to a large didgeridoo, which was really just a long, slightly tapered, hollow piece of wood. Here in the marsh, the fully grown didgeridoos were huge, so it was fairly easy for Talon to crawl inside the instrument's wider end.

'I don't see any clogs,' Talon called from halfway inside.

'I know what I hear, Talon. Please, can you

crawl all the way in? I won't feel happy until I know the whole thing is clear.'

'All the way in?' the Troll repeated. 'Your Majesty, it's a rather tight squeeze . . .'

'I understand,' sighed the Queen. 'So what you're telling me is that you don't really want the Harp that badly . . .'

'All the way in, Your Majesty,' grumbled Talon. 'Consider it done.'

Talon crawled all the way inside the didgeridoo, not stopping until his head poked out of the smaller end. The effect was not unlike a Talon sausage; his head was visible, as were his legs below the knee, but his entire neck, arms and body were squeezed tightly inside the didgeridoo.

'There,' he declared triumphantly. 'Not a single clog.'

'Thank you, Talon,' the Queen beamed.

'You're welcome,' he said. 'Now if you would just give me a hand *out* of the didgeridoo . . .'

'Actually,' grinned the Queen, 'I think you're perfect just the way you are!'

With a tinkling laugh, the Queen turned back into . . .

'Melody!' shrieked Bizzy.

The fairies raced into each other's arms for a giant hug. As they pulled apart, Pinx and Bizzy flooded Melody with questions, but Silky cut them off. There was no time to lose.

Silky and Pinx flew to the grand pianofern where Petal still lay sheltered, but by the time they had carried her back to the other fairies, Talon had managed to stand up. His face red with anger, he screamed a spell in Trollish . . . but nothing happened. With his crystal completely covered by the didgeridoo and his hands pinned inside, Talon was helpless. He could only toddle back and forth, screaming that he'd get his revenge . . . until he fell face-first into a patch of recorder reeds that played a mournful melody in his honour.

The fairies quickly zoomed to the Ladder, arriving just as the Land of Music began to move away. Anxiously, they leaped through the clouds . . . and landed at the top of the Ladder in the Faraway Tree. They had done it. The Faraway Fairies and the Enchanted Harp were safely home at last.

Chapter Twelve

Allegra's Message

'Why did the dragon princess go to the dentist?'

'I don't know, why?

'To get her teeth crowned!'

'WAAAA–HA–HA!' Dido roared with laughter, and her eyes streamed with tears, which Bizzy expertly collected in a mug.

Dido had already spent several hours in the Faraway Fairies' kitchen, with Bizzy constantly telling her jokes, collecting her tears and using them to make dragon-tear tea. Petal had gulped down several mugs of it already, and was sitting in her favourite rocking chair, covered in blankets, and getting the full story from her friends on everything she had missed when she was resting in the grand pianofern.

'Wait,' Petal began, not even believing what she was about to say, 'you mean Melody *flirted* with Talon?'

'She let him kiss her hand!' Silky squealed.

'EEEWWW!' shouted Pinx, Petal and Bizzy in perfect unison.

'I had to!' Melody objected.

'"Oh Talon, darling, please, tell me more about how we'll rule the Enchanted World, side by side,"' Pinx mimicked, batting her eyes.

'I did not say that!' Melody complained.

Now it was Bizzy's turn to affect a high-pitched imitation. She struck a melodramatic pose and cried, '"Oh Talon, how I long to feel your foul, fleshy fingers on my face!"'

'EEEWWW!' the girls chorused again, Melody included, laughing so hard that they could barely breathe.

When they finally recovered, Silky put an arm around Melody.

'You are now officially a quadruple-talent

Twinkletune: a singer, dancer, musician *and* actress,' she said. 'I would never have been able to pull that off.'

'I wasn't sure *I* could, either,' Melody admitted, smiling, 'but I suppose I did a lot of things I wasn't sure I could do.'

'Like what?' demanded Pinx. 'You still haven't told us how you got away from Queen Quadrille and her guards!'

Melody told them everything: about The Game, Allegra, how she had shattered the shatterproof glass, what she had finally discovered about Queen Quadrille, and how the Queen had tackled her, sending them both falling through the trapdoor. They would have been sucked all the way down to the soundproof pit, but Melody had managed to grab a root that stuck out just below the door, and she had held on tightly to both it and the Queen. The Queen had begged Melody to let her go and languish in the pit forever, but

Melody wouldn't do it. Instead, she had managed to transform into a trombone, hooked over the root with the Queen's hand held firmly in her coils. She had played a supremely loud low G sharp, moving her slide with such force that it had kicked the trapdoor open, at which point she had transformed back into herself and asked the guards to help pull them out. After they did so, Melody had begged the people to show mercy to Queen Quadrille. Then she had left to find her friends.

'Really?' marvelled Pinx. 'You asked them to show mercy? After everything she did? After everything she did to her own people?'

'I felt sorry for her,' said Melody with a shrug. 'She hated herself because she never felt good enough to be what everyone expected her to be. It's so sad.'

'I don't know if "sad" is the word I'd use,' mused Silky. 'More like "cruel".'

'Maybe,' admitted Melody, 'but the odd

thing is that if I hadn't got to know her so well, I could never have done a transformation good enough to fool Talon.'

'Um . . . Melody?' Bizzy said, looking a little puzzled. 'Are you expecting a musical note? Because there's one at the window.'

The fairies exchanged looks and flew to the window, where a musical note was indeed trying to get in. Bizzy opened it and the note flew inside, heading straight for Melody. It popped to reveal a small hologram of Allegra!

'Melody, Silky, Bizzy, Petal and Pinx – I miss you all so much!' said the hologram with a grin. 'I know you're all home safe and sound, but I thought you might want to know how much has changed in the Land of Music.'

Allegra's image filled them in on what had been happening. Queen Quadrille's subjects did show her mercy. They stripped her of her powers and exiled her to the Showerlands, a desolate area, but one whose amazing echoing

acoustics made anyone's voice sound beautiful. For possibly the first time in her life, the ex-Queen had a chance to be happy.

When the Queen had gone, all her prisoners were released from the soundproof pits. As Melody had suspected, one of the pits held the previous Queen Quadrille! She was immediately hailed as the ruler of the Land of Music, but she refused. After seeing what her daughter had done, the old Queen changed the rules of the Land. From now on, the election of each new Queen Quadrille would be based on musical talent and kindness to their fellow citizens. The first election was held immediately . . .

'And you'll never believe it; I was named Queen Quadrille!' the Allegra hologram enthused, beating her belly drums and gong back for emphasis. 'I'm re-opening the Land of Music's Conservatory, and Melody, I can't think of anyone who deserves the first invitation more than you. Whenever you can make it, we'll be here waiting.'

Allegra's hologram thanked them all once more, then twittered a tune on her slide-whistle tongue before vanishing into thin air. Silky, Bizzy, Petal and Pinx turned to stare at Melody, who looked rather shocked.

'I was invited to Queen Quadrille's Conservatory,' Melody said.

'It's exactly what you always wanted,' said Silky.

Although they were all thinking the same thing, Bizzy was the first to put it into words.

'So . . . should we be planning a goodbye party?' she asked.

'Sure,' Melody said.

Pinx, Petal, Bizzy and Silky nodded, wanting to be supportive, but their hearts sank. Then Melody grinned.

'Some day,' she finished.

'You mean you're staying?' asked Petal.

'Of course,' said Melody. 'The Conservatory's a dream come true, but nothing's more important than sticking with my best friends and finishing our mission: to save the Enchanted World.'

'Humongous Homecoming Hug!' Bizzy cried, and the five fairies all embraced.

A giant, wracking sob interrupted their thoughts.

'Your friendship . . . it's so beautiful!' wailed Dido from the kitchen.

The fairies laughed and flew off to comfort the dragon (and collect her tears!).

Challenging as the day had been, it became the perfect evening: all five of them just telling stories and making each other laugh out loud – simply being together and enjoying each other's company. They sometimes wished that things could be that way all the time.

But they knew that their next mission was just around the corner. And when it came, they would be ready.

If you can't wait for another exciting
adventure with Silky and her fairy
friends, here's a sneak preview . . .

Enid Blyton's
ENCHANTED
WORLD
Petal and the
Eternal Bloom

For fun and activities, go to
www.blyton.com/enchantedworld

Chapter One

Petal's Room

'Oh honestly, you are impossible,' Petal scolded.

Every other bird, squirrel, chipmunk and tree frog in Petal's room waited its turn for the breakfast crumbs she gave them, but not the raven. The minute he got the chance, he swooped down, pushed everyone else out of the way and devoured as many morsels as possible, triggering screeching protests from the other creatures in the room.

'Enough!' Petal cried. 'Have I ever let any of you miss breakfast?'

One of the difficulties of talking to plants and animals was the noise. Petal's ears buzzed constantly with all kinds of chatter: magpies and starlings nattering about the places they had flown; vines fighting over who was the longest; and diva blooms which clucked in annoyance at anything *daring* to look as beautiful as them.

At times like these, Petal was grateful that she could not read their minds. The very idea of adding their twittering thoughts to the babble of conversation that she could already hear gave her a headache.

'Petal! I need you!' Pinx cried as she soared in from above.

Petal's room had only three walls; the fourth wall and ceiling were wide open to nature, allowing a constant stream of creatures – as well as Petal's fairy friends – to flutter, crawl and skitter in and out.

Pinx was holding a piece of fabric, talking at top speed and poring over the blossoms in Petal's room.

'I was out there trying to make the most fantabulacious sash that just screamed, "WOW!" and it wasn't screaming at all, it was whimpering, and clearly a Pinx sash *cannot* whimper, and then BOOM! it came to me exactly what it needs: flowers! And where can I find the best flowers?' Pinx's eyes widened as she came to a fuzzy, orange-leafed bush with giant blooms bursting with fuchsia and teal. '*Here!*' she cried, and began plucking flowers as quickly as she could.

Petal winced as the bush (whose name was Imogene) gave a shrill scream.

'You tell that fairy she has no right to pick my blooms without asking first! Maybe we should see how she likes it when I snag my thorn on one of her silly dresses!'

'This is perfect, Petal!' Pinx cried. 'Thanks – you're the best!'

'*You're* the best?' Imogene spluttered. 'Did *you* raise thirty-seven flowers from bud to bloom? Did *you* –'

'No, *you* did, Imogene,' said Petal, 'and if you hadn't done such a spectacular job, Pinx wouldn't want your flowers at all. If you ask me, it's a compliment.'

Petal smiled as Imogene stammered, unable to argue with this logic. But her satisfaction was immediately interrupted by . . .

'Petal, prepare for a Piece of Prestidigitation of Preposterously Prodigious Proportions!' Bizzy cried as she flew in.

'What does *that* mean?' Petal asked.

'I have a great new spell!' Bizzy translated, raising her arms with a flourish and making all her bangles rattle. 'Watch as I turn this patch of small flowers into Titanic Towers of Treelike Treasures!'

Bizzy saw Petal's confused look and explained, 'I'm going to make them taller!'

A look of doubt crossed Petal's face.

'That is, if you think they won't mind,' Bizzy added.

'Mind?' a flower cried. 'We'd *love* to be taller!'

The whole patch clamoured for Bizzy to

get on with her spell immediately.

'Go for it,' Petal said.

Bizzy closed her eyes, concentrated and then cried, 'Flahwahh-groo, flahwahh-graa, flahwahh-groodle-oodle-grow!'

'AAAAAHHHHH!' came the horrified screams of thirty blooms.

'Hmmm,' Bizzy winced, looking at her handiwork. 'I don't think I got the spell quite right. Instead of "taller", the flowers got . . .'

'*Tealer*!' the flowers wailed.

The previously yellow blossoms were now a bright shade of greenish-blue that made them look more sickly than beautiful.

'Oh no, here we go again,' sighed a rose.

Petal turned and saw Melody flying in. Melody knew that plants liked music, and she often sang to them. Unfortunately, Melody didn't realise that certain lilies and roses were very particular about the *volume* of the music.

'Can't someone turn her down?' huffed a lily.

'Oh, no!' came a sudden cry from the daffodils.

Silky was flying towards them. Silky adored daffodils, but she had a habit of putting her whole nose deep inside the bloom to inhale its scent . . .

'Hasn't she ever heard of personal space?' cried Daffo, one of the taller blooms.

Petal laughed as she hovered in the middle of her room, surrounded by the squeals of the plants, the background chatter of the animals and the voices of her friends. Life in the Faraway Tree was never dull for a second. It didn't matter to her that there was always a dilemma or an argument taking place somewhere. She was happy to let it all wash over her. It was her ability to remain serene, calm and loyal that made everybody in the Faraway Tree love her.

'AH . . . AH . . . *ACHOOO!*'

The wind from the sneeze blew several of

Imogene's blooms off Pinx's sash.

'My sash!' Pinx cried, zooming into the air with her hands on her hips. 'Whoever did this has about five seconds to confess!'

A giant nose peeked out from between several stalks of bamboo.

'Sorry,' Cluecatcher said as he pushed his way into the room. 'I'm allergic to bamboo.'

Witch Whisper was behind Cluecatcher, and the sight of them made Petal suddenly attentive because she knew ...

'There's a new land at the top of the Tree!' Silky cried.

'Yes,' Witch Whisper confirmed, 'and it's one in which your help, Petal, will be very important.'

'*Me?*' Petal asked.

'It's the Land of Flora,' Cluecatcher said. 'It's populated solely by plants.'

'A Positively Perfect Petal Place!' Bizzy grinned.

'The Talisman there is the Eternal Bloom,'
Witch Whisper continued, 'a beautiful flower
that never wilts. You need to bring it back to
the Vault before the Land moves away from
the Tree . . . and before Talon finds it.'

'Assuming Talon ever escaped the
didgeridoo in the Land of Music,' Melody
giggled.

The other Fairies giggled too . . . until they
noticed Witch Whisper frowning at them.

'Talon is stronger than you think,' she said.
'You have had success against him, but each
success only makes him angrier. He feeds on
that fury, and grows more powerful every
time. I warn you not to underestimate him . . .
or it could be your undoing.'

Witch Whisper smiled and looked into the
eyes of each fairy. They could all see the
confidence that burned there. Despite her
warnings, she had faith that they could
succeed.

'You must get ready,' she said. 'As soon as The Land of Flora settles at the top of the Tree, Talon will start searching for the Eternal Bloom.'

Although Talon did not enter Lands by the Faraway Tree's Ladder, his magical transportation abilities were very limited. He could only magic himself into a Land that had stopped moving, and there was only one thing that could attach itself to a Land and make it stop – the Faraway Tree.

'So . . . are you ready?' Witch Whisper asked.

Petal thought about the Land of Flora. It was exactly the kind of place that she had dreamed of visiting when Silky first told her about the mission, and she felt a shiver of excitement race through her body. She beamed at Witch Whisper.

'I can't wait,' she said.